Glooscap
and the Baby

A Native American story from the Wabanaki people

Retold by Caroline Walker

and illustrated by Teresa Martinez

W
FRANKLIN WATTS
LONDON•SYDNEY

Chapter 1

In the Old Time, not long after the world was made, there was a great hero called Glooscap. Some people say he descended from the Great Spirit that created the world.

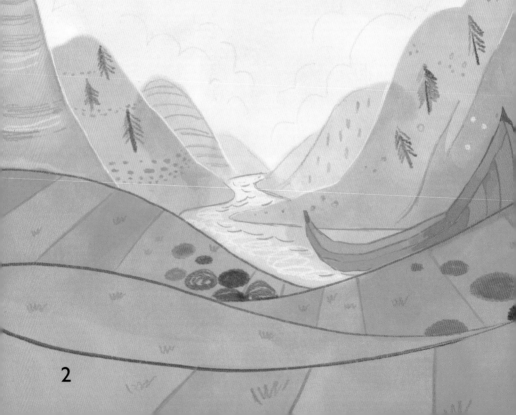

3

Glooscap was strong. He protected the Wabanaki people. He defeated the wicked giants and spirits who scared them.

Glooscap was also wise. He taught
the Wabanaki people which animals and plants
to eat. He showed them which barks and leaves
to use for medicine. He told them the names of
all the stars. The people loved Glooscap.

Chapter 2

Glooscap was proud of his great strength and wisdom.

"I am a great hero," he said to himself. "I can conquer anything!"

An old woman heard what he said.

"Are you sure?" she asked him.

9

Glooscap was surprised.

"Do you not know?" he asked. "I have conquered all the giants and the spirits. There is nothing left to defeat."

The old woman smiled.

"I know a creature called a Wasis," she replied. "He seems small and weak, but I don't think you can defeat him."

"Take me to him," said Glooscap, boldly. "I will defeat him like I have defeated all the others."

The old woman took Glooscap to her tepee.

"Here is the Wasis," she said. She pointed towards the floor.

Glooscap saw a small baby sitting on the floor.

All the baby said was "Goo, goo."

Chapter 3

"Ha!" said Glooscap.

He saw that the Wasis was very small.

The Wasis didn't have any armour or special

powers. It would be easy for Glooscap

to tell him what to do.

"Come here!" Glooscap said to the Wasis.

"Come here, now!"

The Wasis looked at Glooscap, but he didn't
go to him. He didn't move at all.

He just said "goo, goo," and sucked his thumb.

"He won't come to you," the old woman said.

"Now what will you do?"

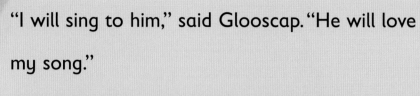

"I will sing to him," said Glooscap. "He will love my song."

Glooscap started to sing a beautiful song. It was so beautiful that all the animals in the forest stopped still and listened.

But the Wasis didn't like the song.

He did not clap or cheer.

He just yawned and shook his rattle.

Chapter 4

Glooscap pulled his magic flute from his bag and started to play. The music made some snakes come in from the forest. They hissed and slithered all around the tepee

The Wasis saw the snakes, but he was not afraid. He just giggled and shook his rattle.

Glooscap stopped playing his flute and the snakes slithered away.

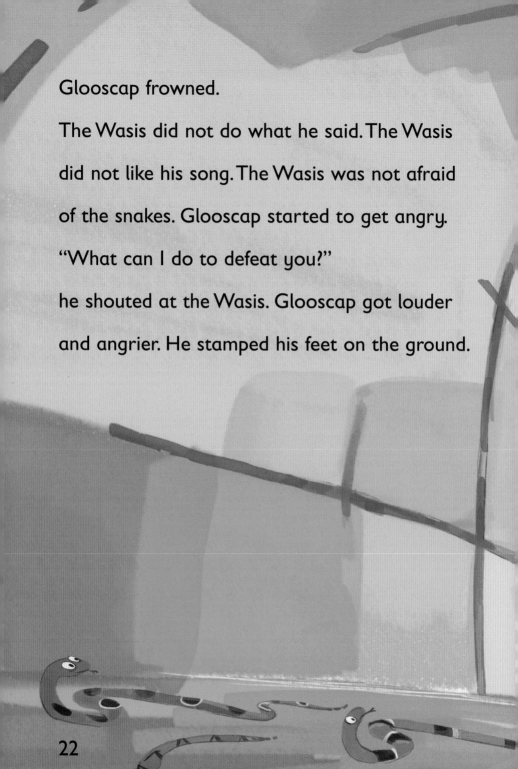

Glooscap frowned.

The Wasis did not do what he said. The Wasis did not like his song. The Wasis was not afraid of the snakes. Glooscap started to get angry. "What can I do to defeat you?"

he shouted at the Wasis. Glooscap got louder and angrier. He stamped his feet on the ground.

When Glooscap shouted, the Wasis began to cry.

"Be quiet!" Glooscap shouted as loud as he could.

But the Wasis cried louder and louder.

The Wasis could cry much louder than

Glooscap could shout, even though

he was very small.

Glooscap put his hands over his ears.

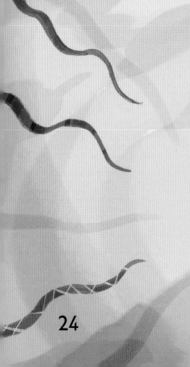

Chapter 5

"I've had enough," cried Glooscap. "I can't defeat this strange creature!" and Glooscap ran out of the tepee.

The old woman smiled.

"Glooscap might be a great hero, but he can't defeat the little Wasis."

The old woman shook the rattle and the Wasis stopped crying. He lay on his mat and gurgled. "Goo, goo," he said. "Goo, goo."

To this day, babies say "goo, goo." Some people wonder if they are remembering the time when the mighty Glooscap was defeated by the little Wasis.

Things to think about

1. What words best decribe Glooscap?
2. Why does the woman challenge Glooscap?
3. How does Glooscap try to defeat the little Wasis?
4. What do you think Glooscap learns from the Wasis?
5. Can you think of any other stories in which a boastful character meets their match?

Write it yourself

One of the themes in this story is how boastful people often find that they are not as mighty as they think thy are. Now try to write your own story about a similar theme.

Plan your story before you begin to write it.
Start off with a story map:

- a beginning to introduce the characters and where your story is set (the setting);
- a problem which the main characters will need to fix in the story;
- an ending where the problems are resolved.

Get writing! Try to use interesting phrases such as "stamped his feet" to make your characters come alive and excite your reader.

Notes for parents and carers

Independent reading

This series is designed to provide an opportunity for your child to read independently, for pleasure and enjoyment. These notes are written for you to help your child make the most of this book.

About the book

Glooscap is a mighty giant who can defeat anything ... or so he thinks. When an old woman challenges the boastful Glooscap to defeat the Wasis, he is in for a shock! The Wasis does not fear anyone ...

Before reading

Ask your child why they have selected this book. Look at the title and blurb together. What do they think it will be about? Do they think they will like it?

During reading

Encourage your child to read independently. If they get stuck on a word, remind them that they can sound it out in syllable chunks. They can also read on in the sentence and think about what would make sense.

After reading

Support comprehension and help your child think about the messages in the book that go beyond the story, using the questions on the page opposite. Give your child a chance to respond to the story, asking:

- Did you enjoy the story and why?
- Who was your favourite character?
- What was your favourite part?
- What did you expect to happen at the end?

Franklin Watts
First published in Great Britain in 2020

Copyright © The Watts Publishing Group 2020
All rights reserved.

Series Editors: Jackie Hamley and Melanie Palmer
Series Advisors: Dr Sue Bodman and Glen Franklin
Series Designers: Cathryn Gilbert and Peter Scoulding

A CIP catalogue record for this book is
available from the British Library.

ISBN 978 1 4451 7252 1 (hbk)
ISBN 978 1 4451 7257 6 (pbk)
ISBN 978 1 4451 7261 3 (library ebook)
ISBN 978 1 4451 8086 1 (ebook)

Printed in China

Franklin Watts
An imprint of
Hachette Children's Group
Part of The Watts Publishing Group
Carmelite House
50 Victoria Embankment
London EC4Y 0DZ

An Hachette UK Company
www.hachette.co.uk

www.franklinwatts.co.uk